THROUGH THE GATES *of the* SILVER KEY

H. P. Lovecraft

&

E. Hoffmann Price

Pharos Books

HB ISBN: 978-93-71411-07-3
ISBN: 978-93-59836-29-4
eISBN: 978-93-59832-30-2

Publisher: Pharos Books (P) Ltd.
Plot No.-63, 1st Floor, Main Mother Dairy Road
Pandav Nagar, East Delhi-110092
Phone: 011-40395855, +4049916623
WhatsApp: +91 9319228272
E-mail: bookspharos@gmail.com
Website: www.pharosbooks.in
Edition: 2025

Printed By: Sushma Book Binding House, Okhla Industrial Area, Phase II, New Delhi-110020

Through the Gates of the Silver Key
H. P. Lovecraft & E. Hoffmann Price

CONTENTS

Through the Gates of the Silver Key

CHAPTER 1

In a vast room hung with strangely figured arras and carpeted with Boukhara rugs of impressive age and workmanship, four men were sitting around a document-strown table. From the far corners, where odd tripods of wrought iron were now and then replenished by an incredibly aged negro in somber livery, came the hypnotic fumes of olibanum; while in a deep niche on one side there ticked a curious, coffin-shaped clock whose dial bore baffling hieroglyphs and whose four hands did not move in consonance with any time system known on this planet. It was a singular and disturbing room, but well fitted to the business then at hand. For there, in the New Orleans home of this continent's greatest mystic, mathematician and orientalist, there was being settled at last the estate of a scarcely less great mystic, scholar, author and dreamer who had vanished from the face of the earth four years before.

Randolph Carter, who had all his life sought to escape from the tedium and limitations of waking reality in the beckoning vistas of dreams and fabled avenues of other dimensions, disappeared from the sight of man on the seventh of October, 1928, at the age of fifty-four. His career had been a strange and lonely one, and there were those who inferred from his curious novels many episodes more bizarre than any in his recorded history. His association with Harley Warren, the South Carolina mystic whose studies in the primal Naacal language of the Himalayan priests had led to such outrageous conclusions, had been close. Indeed, it was he who—one mist-mad, terrible night in an ancient graveyard—had seen Warren descend into a dank and nitrous vault, never to emerge. Carter lived in Boston, but it was from the wild, haunted hills behind hoary and witch-accursed Arkham that all his forebears had come. And it was amid these ancient, cryptically brooding hills that he had ultimately vanished.

His old servant, Parks—who died early in 1930—had spoken of the strangely aromatic and hideously carven box he had found in the attic, and of the undecipherable parchments and queerly figured silver key which that box had contained: matters of which Carter had also written to others. Carter, he said, had told him that this key had come down from his ancestors, and that it would help him to unlock the gates to his lost boyhood, and to strange dimensions and fantastic realms which he had hitherto visited only in vague, brief and elusive dreams. Then one day Carter took the box and its contents and rode away in his car, never to return.

Later on, people found the car at the side of an old, grass-grown road in the hills behind crumbling Arkham—the hills where Carter's forebears had once dwelt, and where the ruined cellar of the great Carter homestead still gaped to the sky. It was in a grove of tall elms near by that another of the Carters had mysteriously vanished in 1781, and not far away was the half-rotted cottage where Goody Fowler, the witch, had brewed her ominous potions still earlier. The region had been settled in 1692 by fugitives from the witchcraft trials in Salem, and even now it bore a name for vaguely ominous things scarcely to be envisaged. Edmund Carter had fled from the shadow of Gallows Hill just in time, and the tales of his sorceries were many. Now, it seemed, his lone descendant had gone somewhere to join him!

In the car they found the hideously carved box of fragrant wood, and the parchment which no man could read. The silver key was gone—presumably with Carter. Further than that there was no certain clue. Detectives from Boston said that the fallen timbers of the old Carter place seemed oddly disturbed, and somebody found a handkerchief on the rock-ridged, sinisterly wooded slope behind the ruins near the dreaded cave called the Snake Den.

It was then that the country legends about the Snake Den gained a new vitality. Farmers whispered of the blasphemous uses to which old Edmund Carter the wizard had put that horrible grotto, and added later tales about the fondness which Randolph Carter himself had had for it when a boy. In Carter's boyhood the venerable gambrel-roofed homestead was still standing and tenanted by his great-uncle Christopher. He had visited there often, and had talked singularly about the Snake Den. People remembered what he had said about a deep fissure and an unknown inner cave beyond, and speculated on the change he had shown after spending one whole memorable day in the cavern when he was nine. That was in October, too—and ever after that he had seemed to have an uncanny knack at prophesying future events.

It had rained late in the night that Carter vanished, and no one was quite able to trace his footprints from the car. Inside the Snake Den all was amorphous liquid mud, owing to the copious seepage. Only the ignorant rustics whispered about the prints they thought they spied where the great elms overhang the road, and on the sinister hillside near the Snake Den, where the handkerchief was found. Who could pay attention to whispers that spoke of stubby little tracks like those which Randolph Carter's square-toed boots made when he was a small boy? It was as crazy a notion as that other whisper—that the tracks of old Benijah Corey's peculiar heelless boots had met the stubby little tracks in the road. Old Benijah had been the Carters' hired man when Randolph was young; but he had died thirty years ago.

It must have been these whispers—plus Carter's own statement to Parks and others that the queerly arabesqued silver key would help him unlock the gates of his lost boyhood—which caused a number of mystical students to declare that the missing man had actually doubled back on the trail of time and returned through forty-five years to that other October day in 1883 when he had stayed in the Snake Den as a small boy. When he came out that night, they argued, he had somehow made the whole trip to 1928 and back; for did he not thereafter know of things which were to happen later? And yet he had never spoken of anything to happen after 1928.

One student—an elderly eccentric of Providence, Rhode Island, who had enjoyed a long and close correspondence with Carter—had a still more elaborate theory, and believed that Carter had not only returned to boyhood, but achieved a further liberation, roving at will through the prismatic vistas of boyhood dream. After a strange vision this man published a tale of Carter's vanishing in which he hinted that the lost one now reigned as king on the opal throne of Ilek-Vad, that fabulous town of turrets atop the hollow cliffs of glass overlooking the twilight sea wherein the bearded and finny Gnorri build their singular labyrinths.

It was this old man, Ward Phillips, who pleaded most loudly against the apportionment of Carter's estate to his heirs—all distant cousins—on the ground that he was still alive in another time-dimension and might well return some day. Against him was arrayed the legal talent of one of the cousins, Ernest K.

Aspinwall of Chicago, a man ten years Carter's senior, but keen as a youth in forensic battles. For four years the contest had raged, but now the time for apportionment had come, and this vast, strange room in New Orleans was to be the scene of the arrangements.

It was the home of Carter's literary and financial executor—the distinguished Creole student of mysteries and Eastern antiquities, Etienne-Laurent de Marigny. Carter had met de Marigny during the war, when they both served in the French Foreign Legion, and had at once cleaved to him because of their similar tastes and outlook. When, on a memorable joint furlough, the learned young Creole had taken the wistful Boston dreamer to Bayonne, in the south of France, and had shown him certain terrible secrets in the nighted and immemorial crypts that burrow beneath that brooding, eon-weighted city, the friendship was forever sealed. Carter's will had named de Marigny as executor, and now that avid scholar was reluctantly presiding over the settlement of the estate. It was sad work for him, for like the old Rhode Islander he did not believe that Carter was dead. But what weight have the dreams of mystics against the harsh wisdom of the world?

Around the table in that strange room in the old French Quarter sat the men who claimed an interest in the proceedings. There had been the usual legal advertisements of the conference in papers wherever Carter's heirs were thought to live; yet only four now sat listening to the abnormal ticking of that coffin-shaped clock which told no earthly time, and to the bubbling of the courtyard fountain beyond half-curtained, fan-lighted windows. As the hours wore on, the faces of the four were half shrouded in the curling fumes from the tripods, which, piled recklessly with fuel, seemed to need less and less attention from the silently gliding and increasingly nervous old negro.

There was Etienne de Marigny himself—slim, dark, handsome, mustached, and still young. Aspinwall, representing the heirs, was white-haired, apoplectic-faced, side-whiskered, and portly. Phillips, the Providence mystic, was lean, gray, long-nosed, clean-shaven, and stoop-shouldered. The fourth man was non-committal in age—lean, with a dark, bearded, singularly immobile face of very regular contour, bound with the turban of a high-caste Brahman and having night-black, burning, almost irisless eyes which seemed to gaze out from a vast distance behind the features. He had announced himself as the Swami Chandraputra, an adept from Benares, with important information to give; and both de Marigny and Phillips—who had corresponded with him—had been quick to recognize the genuineness of his mystical pretensions. His speech had an oddly forced, hollow, metallic quality, as if the use of English taxed his vocal apparatus; yet his language was as easy, correct and idiomatic as any native Anglo-Saxon's. In general attire he was the normal European civilian, but his loose clothes sat peculiarly badly on him, while his bushy black beard, Eastern turban, and large, white mittens gave him an air of exotic eccentricity.

De Marigny, fingering the parchment found in Carter's car, was speaking.

"No, I have not been able to make anything of the parchment. Mr. Phillips, here, also gives it up. Colonel Churchward declares it is not Naacal, and it looks nothing at all like the hieroglyphics on that Easter Island war-club. The carvings on that box, though, do strongly suggest Easter Island images. The nearest thing I can recall to these parchment characters—notice how all the letters seem to hang down from horizontal word-bars—is the writing in a book poor Harley Warren once had. It came from India while Carter and I were visiting him in 1919, and he never would tell us anything about it—said it would be better if we didn't know, and hinted that it might have come originally from some place other than the Earth. He took it with him in December, when he went down into the vault in that old graveyard—but neither he nor the book ever came to the surface again. Some time ago I sent our friend here—the Swami Chandraputra—a memory-sketch of some of those letters, and also a photostatic copy of the Carter parchment. He believes he may be able to shed light on them after certain references and consultations.

"But the key—Carter sent me a photograph of that. Its curious arabesques were not letters, but seem to have belonged to the same culture-tradition as the parchment. Carter always spoke of being on the point of solving the mystery, though he never gave details. Once he grew almost poetic about the whole business. That antique silver key, he said, would unlock the successive doors that bar our free march down the mighty corridors of space and time to the very Border which no man has crossed since Shaddad with his terrific genius built and concealed in the sands of Arabia Petræa the prodigious domes and uncounted minarets of thousand-pillared Irem. Half-starved darvishes—wrote Carter—and thirst-crazed nomads have returned to tell of that monumental portal, and of the hand that is sculptured above the keystone of the arch, but no man has passed and retraced his steps to say that his footprints on the garnet-strown sands within bear witness to his visit. The key, he surmised, was that for which the cyclopean sculptured hand vainly grasps.

"Why Carter didn't take the parchment as well as the key, we can not say. Perhaps he forgot it—or perhaps he forbore to take it through recollection of one who had taken a book of like characters into a vault and never returned. Or perhaps it was really immaterial to what he wished to do."

As de Marigny paused, old Mr. Phillips spoke in a harsh, shrill voice.

"We can know of Randolph Carter's wandering only what we dream. I have been to many strange places in dreams, and have heard many strange and significant things in Ulthar, beyond the River Skai. It does not appear that the parchment was needed, for certainly Carter re-entered the world of his boyhood dreams, and is now a king in Ilek-Vad."

Mr. Aspinwall grew doubly apoplectic-looking as he sputtered: "Can't somebody shut that old fool up? We've had enough of these moonings. The problem is to divide the property, and it's about time we got to it."

For the first time Swami Chandraputra spoke in his queerly alien voice.

"Gentlemen, there is more to this matter than you think. Mr. Aspinwall does not do well to laugh at the evidence of dreams. Mr. Phillips has taken an incomplete view—perhaps because he has not dreamed enough. I, myself, have done much dreaming. We in India have always done that, just as all the Carters seem to have done it. You, Mr. Aspinwall, as a maternal cousin, are naturally not a Carter. My own dreams, and certain other sources of information, have told me a great deal which you still find obscure. For example, Randolph Carter forgot that parchment which he couldn't decipher—yet it would have been well for him had he remembered to take it. You see, I have really learned pretty much what happened to Carter after he left his car with the silver key at sunset on that seventh of October, four years ago."

Aspinwall audibly sneered, but the others sat up with heightened interest. The smoke from the tripods increased, and the crazy ticking of that coffin-shaped clock seemed to fall into bizarre patterns like the dots and dashes of some alien and insoluble telegraph message from outer space. The Hindoo leaned back, half closed his eyes, and continued in that oddly labored yet idiomatic speech, while before his audience there began to float a picture of what had happened to Randolph Carter.

CHAPTER 2

The hills beyond Arkham are full of a strange magic—something, perhaps, which the old wizard Edmund Carter called down from the stars and up from the crypts of nether earth when he fled there from Salem in 1692. As soon as Randolph Carter was back among them he knew that he was close to one of the gates which a few audacious, abhorred and alien-souled men have blasted through titan walls betwixt the world and the outside absolute. Here, he felt, and on this day of the year, he could carry out with success the message he had deciphered months before from the arabesques of that tarnished and incredibly ancient silver key. He knew now how it must be rotated, and how it must be held up to the setting sun, and what syllables of ceremony must be intoned into the void at the ninth and last turning. In a spot as close to a dark polarity and induced gate as this, it could not fail in its primary functions. Certainly, he would rest that night in the lost boyhood for which he had never ceased to mourn.

He got out of the car with the key in his pocket, walking uphill deeper and deeper into the shadowy core of that brooding, haunted countryside of winding road, vine-grown stone wall, black woodland, gnarled, neglected orchard, gaping-windowed, deserted farmhouse, and nameless ruin. At the sunset hour, when the distant spires of Kingsport gleamed in the ruddy blaze, he took out the key and made the needed turnings and intonations. Only later did he realize how soon the ritual had taken effect.

Then in the deepening twilight he had heard a voice out of the past: Old Benijah Corey, his great-uncle's hired man. Had not old Benijah been dead for thirty years? Thirty years before *when*? What was time? Where had he been? Why was it strange that Benijah should be calling him on this seventh of October, 1883? Was he not out later than Aunt Martha had told him to stay? What was this key in his blouse pocket, where his little telescope—given him by his father on his ninth birthday, two months before—ought to be? Had he found it in the attic at home? Would it unlock the mystic pylon which his sharp eye had traced amidst the jagged rocks at the back of that inner cave behind the Snake Den on the hill? That was the place they always coupled with old Edmund Carter the wizard. People wouldn't go there, and nobody but him had ever noticed or squirmed through the root-choked fissure to that great black inner chamber with the pylon. Whose hands had carved that hint of a pylon out of the living rock? Old Wizard Edmund's—or *others* that he had conjured up and commanded?

That evening little Randolph ate supper with Uncle Chris and Aunt Martha in the old gambrel-roofed farmhouse.

Next morning he was up early and out through the twisted-boughed apple orchard to the upper timber-lot where the mouth of the Snake Den lurked black and forbidding amongst grotesque, over-nourished oaks. A nameless expectancy was upon him, and he did not even notice the loss of his handkerchief as he fumbled in his blouse pocket to see if the queer silver key was safe. He crawled through the dark orifice with tense, adventurous assurance, lighting his way with matches taken from the sitting-room. In another moment he had wriggled through the root-choked fissure at the farther end, and was in the vast, unknown inner grotto whose ultimate rock wall seemed half like a monstrous and consciously shapen pylon. Before that dank, dripping wall he stood silent and awestruck, lighting one match after another as he gazed. Was that stony bulge above the keystone of the imagined arch really a gigantic sculptured hand? Then he drew forth the silver key, and made motions and intonations whose source he could only dimly remember. Was anything forgotten? He knew only that he wished to cross the barrier to the untrammelled land of his dreams and the gulfs where all dimensions dissolved in the absolute.

CHAPTER 3

What happened then is scarcely to be described in words. It is full of those paradoxes, contradictions and anomalies which have no place in waking life, but which fill our more fantastic dreams and are taken as matters of course till we return to our narrow, rigid, objective world of limited causation and tri-dimensional logic. As the Hindoo continued his tale, he had difficulty in avoiding what seemed—even more than the notion of a man transferred through the years to boyhood—an air of trivial, puerile extravagance. Mr. Aspinwall, in disgust, gave an apoplectic snort and virtually stopped listening.

For the rite of the silver key, as practised by Randolph Carter in that black, haunted cave within a cave, did not prove unavailing. From the first gesture and syllable an aura of strange, awesome mutation was apparent—a sense of incalculable disturbance and confusion in time and space, yet one which held no hint of what we recognize as motion and duration. Imperceptibly, such things as age and location ceased to have any significance whatever. The day before, Randolph Carter had miraculously leaped a gulf of years. Now there was no distinction between boy and man. There was only the entity Randolph Carter, with a certain store of images which had lost all connection with terrestrial scenes and circumstances of acquisition. A moment before, there had been an inner cave with vague suggestions of a monstrous arch and gigantic sculptured hand on the farther wall. Now there was neither cave nor absence of cave; neither wall nor absence of wall. There was only a flux of impressions not so much visual as cerebral, amidst which the entity that was Randolph Carter experienced perceptions or registrations of all that his mind revolved on, yet without any clear consciousness of the way in which he received them.

By the time the rite was over, Carter knew that he was in no region whose place could be told by Earth's geographers, and in no age whose date history could fix; for the nature of what was happening was not wholly unfamiliar to him. There were hints of it in the cryptical Pnakotic fragments, and a whole chapter in the forbidden *Necronomicon* of the mad Arab, Abdul Alhazred, had taken on significance when he had deciphered the designs graven on the silver key. A gate had been unlocked—not, indeed, the Ultimate Gate, but one leading from Earth and time to that extension of Earth which is outside time, and from which in turn the Ultimate Gate leads fearsomely and perilously to the Last Void which is outside all earths, all universes, and all matter.

There would be a Guide—and a very terrible one; a Guide who had been an entity of Earth millions of years before, when man was undreamed of, and when forgotten shapes moved on a steaming planet building strange cities among whose last, crumbling ruins the first mammals were to play. Carter remembered what the monstrous *Necronomicon* had vaguely and disconcertingly adumbrated concerning that Guide:

"And while there are those," *the mad Arab had written,* "who have dared to seek glimpses beyond the Veil, and to accept HIM as guide, they would have been more prudent had they avoided commerce with HIM; for it is written in the Book of Thoth how terrific is the price of a single glimpse. Nor may those who pass ever return, for in the vastnesses transcending our world are shapes of darkness that seize and bind. The Affair that shambleth about in the night, the evil that defieth the Elder Sign, the Herd that stand watch at the secret portal each tomb is known to have, and that thrive on that which groweth out of the tenants thereof:—all these Blacknesses are lesser than HE WHO guardeth the Gateway: HE WHO will guide the rash one beyond all the worlds into the Abyss of unnamable devourers. For HE is 'UMR AT-TAWIL, the Most Ancient One, which the scribe rendereth as THE PROLONGED OF LIFE."

Memory and imagination shaped dim half-pictures with uncertain outlines amidst the seething chaos, but Carter knew that they were of memory and imagination only. Yet he felt that it was not chance which built these things in his consciousness, but rather some vast reality, ineffable and undimensioned, which surrounded him and strove to translate itself into the only symbols he was capable of grasping. For no mind of Earth may grasp the extensions of shape which interweave in the oblique gulfs outside time and the dimensions we know.

There floated before Carter a cloudy pageantry of shapes and scenes which he somehow linked with Earth's primal, eon-forgotten past. Monstrous living things moved deliberately through vistas of fantastic handiwork that no sane dream ever held, and landscapes bore incredible vegetation and cliffs and mountains and masonry of no human pattern. There were cities under the sea, and denizens thereof; and towers in great deserts where globes and cylinders and nameless winged entities shot off into space, or hurtled down out of space. All this Carter grasped, though the images bore no fixed relation to one another or to him. He himself had no stable form or position, but only such shifting hints of form and position as his whirling fancy supplied.

He had wished to find the enchanted regions of his boyhood dreams, where galleys sail up the river Oukranos past the gilded spires of Thran, and elephant caravans tramp through perfumed jungles in Kled, beyond forgotten palaces with veined ivory columns that sleep lovely and unbroken under the moon. Now, intoxicated with wider visions, he scarcely knew what he sought. Thoughts of infinite and blasphemous daring rose in his mind, and he knew he would face the dreaded Guide without fear, asking monstrous and terrible things of him.

All at once the pageant of impressions seemed to achieve a vague kind of stabilization. There were great masses of towering stone, carven into alien and incomprehensible designs and disposed according to the laws of some unknown, inverse geometry. Light filtered down from a sky of no assignable color in baffling, contradictory directions, and played almost sentiently over what seemed to be a curved line of gigantic hieroglyphed pedestals more hexagonal than otherwise, and surmounted by cloaked, ill-defined shapes.

There was another shape, too, which occupied no pedestal, but which seemed to glide or float over the cloudy, floor-like lower level. It was not exactly permanent in outline, but held transient suggestions of something remotely preceding or paralleling the human form, though half as large again as an ordinary man. It seemed to be heavily cloaked, like the shapes on the pedestals, with some neutral-colored fabric; and Carter could not detect any eye-holes through which it might gaze. Probably it did not need to gaze, for it seemed to belong to an order of beings far outside the merely physical in organization and faculties.

A moment later Carter knew that this was so, for the Shape had spoken to his mind without sound or language. And though the name it uttered was a dreaded and terrible one, Randolph Carter did not flinch in fear. Instead, he spoke back, equally without sound or language, and made those obeisances which the hideous *Necronomicon* had taught him to make. For this shape was nothing less than that which all the world has feared since Lomar rose out of the sea, and the Children of the Fire Mist came to Earth to teach the Elder Lore to man. It was indeed the frightful Guide and Guardian of the Gate—'UMR AT-TAWIL, the ancient one, which the scribe rendereth the PROLONGED OF LIFE.

The Guide knew, as he knew all things, of Carter's quest and coming, and that this seeker of dreams and secrets stood before him unafraid. There was no horror or malignity in what he radiated, and Carter wondered for a moment whether the mad Arab's terrific blasphemous hints came from envy and a baffled wish to do what was now about to be done. Or perhaps the Guide reserved his horror and malignity for those who feared. As the radiations continued, Carter eventually interpreted them in the form of words.

"I am indeed that Most Ancient One," said the Guide, "of whom you know. We have awaited you—the Ancient Ones and I. You are welcome, even though long delayed. You have the key, and have unlocked the First Gate. Now the Ultimate Gate is ready for your trial. If you fear, you need not advance. You may still go back unharmed, the way you came. But if you choose to advance—"

The pause was ominous, but the radiations continued to be friendly. Carter hesitated not a moment, for a burning curiosity drove him on.

"I will advance," he radiated back, "and I accept you as my Guide."

At this reply the Guide seemed to make a sign by certain motions of his robe which may or may not have involved the lifting of an arm or some homologous member. A second sign followed, and from his well-learned lore Carter knew that he was at last very close to the Ultimate Gate. The light now changed to another inexplicable color, and the shapes on the quasi-hexagonal pedestals became more clearly defined. As they sat more erect, their outlines became more like those of men, though Carter knew that they could not be men. Upon their cloaked heads there now seemed to rest tall, uncertainly colored miters, strangely suggestive of those on certain nameless figures chiselled by a forgotten sculptor along the living cliffs of a high, forbidden mountain in Tartary; while grasped in certain folds of their swathings were long scepters whose carven heads bodied forth a grotesque and archaic mystery.

Carter guessed what they were and whence they came, and Whom they served; and guessed, too, the price of their service. But he was still content, for at one mighty venture he was to learn all. Damnation, he reflected, is but a word bandied about by those whose blindness leads them to condemn all who can see, even with a single eye. He wondered at the vast conceit of those who had babbled of the *malignant* Ancient Ones, as if They could pause from their everlasting dreams to wreak a wrath on mankind. As well, he thought, might a mammoth pause to visit frantic vengeance on an angleworm. Now the whole assemblage on the vaguely hexagonal pillars was greeting him with a gesture of those oddly carven scepters and radiating a message which he understood:

"We salute you, Most Ancient One, and you, Randolph Carter, whose daring has made you one of us."

Carter saw now that one of the pedestals was vacant, and a gesture of the Most Ancient One told him it was reserved for him. He saw also another pedestal, taller than the rest, and at the center of the oddly curved line—neither semicircle nor ellipse, parabola nor hyperbola—which they formed. This, he guessed, was the Guide's own throne. Moving and rising in a manner hardly definable, Carter took his seat; and as he did so he saw that the Guide had seated himself.

Gradually and mistily it became apparent that the Most Ancient One was holding something—some object clutched in the outflung folds of his robe as if for the sight, or what answered for sight, of the cloaked Companions. It was a large sphere, or apparent sphere, of some obscurely iridescent metal, and as the Guide put it forward a low, pervasive half-impression of *sound* began to rise and fall in intervals which seemed to be rhythmic even though they followed no rhythm of Earth. There was a suggestion of chanting—or what human imagination might interpret as chanting. Presently the quasi-sphere began to grow luminous, and as it gleamed up into a cold, pulsating light of unassignable color, Carter saw that its flickerings conformed to the alien rhythm of the chant. Then all the mitered, scepter-bearing Shapes on the pedestals commenced a slight, curious swaying in the same inexplicable rhythm, while nimbuses of unclassifiable light—resembling that of the quasi-sphere—played around their shrouded heads.

The Hindoo paused in his tale and looked curiously at the tall, coffin-shaped clock with the four hands and hieroglyphed dial, whose crazy ticking followed no known rhythm of Earth.

"You, Mr. de Marigny," he suddenly said to his learned host, "do not need to be told the particularly alien rhythm to which those cowled Shapes on the hexagonal pillars chanted and nodded. You are the only one else—in America—who has had a taste of the Outer Extension. That clock—I suppose it was sent you by the Yogi poor Harley Warren used to talk about—the seer who said that he alone of living men had been to Yian-Ho, the hidden legacy of eon-old Leng, and had borne certain things away from that dreadful and forbidden city. I wonder how many of its subtler properties you know? If my dreams and readings be correct, it was made by those who knew much of the First Gateway. But let me go on with my tale."

At last, continued the Swami, the swaying and the suggestion of chanting ceased, the lambent nimbuses around the now drooping and motionless heads faded, while the cloaked shapes slumped curiously on their pedestals. The quasi-sphere, however, continued to pulsate with inexplicable light. Carter felt that the Ancient Ones were sleeping as they had been when he first saw them, and he wondered out of what cosmic dreams his coming had aroused them. Slowly there filtered into his mind the truth that this strange chanting ritual had been one of instruction, and that the Companions had been chanted by the Most Ancient One into a new and peculiar kind of sleep in order that their dreams might open the Ultimate Gate to which the silver key was a passport. He knew that in the profundity of this deep sleep they were contemplating unplumbed vastnesses of utter and absolute outsideness, and that they were to accomplish that which his presence had demanded.

The Guide did not share this sleep, but seemed still to be giving instructions in some subtle, soundless way. Evidently he was implanting images of those things which he wished the Companions to dream: and Carter knew that as each of the Ancient Ones pictured the prescribed thought, there would be born the nucleus of a manifestation visible to his earthly eyes. When the dreams of all the Shapes had achieved a oneness, that manifestation would occur, and everything he required be materialized, through concentration. He had seen such things on Earth—in India, where the combined, projected will of a circle of adepts can make a thought take tangible substance, and in hoary Atlaanât, of which few even dare speak.

Just what the Ultimate Gate was, and how it was to be passed, Carter could not be certain; but a feeling of tense expectancy surged over him. He was conscious of having a kind of body, and of holding the fateful silver key in his hand. The masses of towering stone opposite him seemed to possess the evenness of a wall, toward the center of which his eyes were irresistibly drawn. And then suddenly he felt the mental currents of the Most Ancient One cease to flow forth.

For the first time Carter realized how terrific utter silence, mental and physical, may be. The earlier moments had never failed to contain some perceptible rhythm, if only the faint, cryptical pulse of the Earth's dimensional extension, but now the hush of the abyss seemed to fall upon everything. Despite his intimations of body, he had no audible breath; and the glow of 'Umr at-Tawil's quasi-sphere had grown petrifiedly fixed and unpulsating. A potent nimbus, brighter than those which had played round the heads of the Shapes, blazed frozenly over the shrouded skull of the terrible Guide.

A dizziness assailed Carter, and his sense of lost orientation waxed a thousandfold. The strange lights seemed to hold the quality of the most impenetrable blacknesses heaped upon blacknesses, while about the Ancient Ones, so close on their pseudo-hexagonal thrones, there hovered an air of the most stupefying remoteness. Then he felt himself wafted into immeasurable depths, with waves of perfumed warmth lapping against his face. It was as if he floated in a torrid, rose-tinctured sea; a sea of drugged wine whose waves broke foaming against shores of brazen fire. A great fear clutched him as he half saw that vast expanse of surging sea lapping against its far-off coast. But the moment of silence was broken—the surgings were speaking to him in a language that was not of physical sound or articulate words.

"The Man of Truth is beyond good and evil," *intoned a voice that was not a voice.* "The Man of Truth has ridden to All-Is-One. The Man of Truth has learned that Illusion is the One Reality, and that Substance is the Great Impostor."

And now, in that rise of masonry to which his eyes had been so irresistibly drawn, there appeared the outline of a titanic arch not unlike that which he thought he had glimpsed so long ago in that cave within a cave, on the far, unreal surface of the three-dimensioned Earth. He realised that he had been using the silver key—moving it in accord with an unlearned and instinctive ritual closely akin to that which had opened the Inner Gate. That rose-drunken sea which lapped his cheeks was, he realized, no more or less than the adamantine mass of the solid wall yielding before his spell, and the vortex of thought with which the Ancient Ones had aided his spell. Still guided by instinct and blind determination, he floated forward—and through the Ultimate Gate.

CHAPTER 4

Randolph Carter's advance through that cyclopean bulk of masonry was like a dizzy precipitation through the measureless gulfs between the stars. From a great distance he felt triumphant, god-like surges of deadly sweetness, and after that the rustling of great wings, and impressions of sound like the chirpings and murmurings of objects unknown on Earth or in the solar system. Glancing backward, he saw not one gate alone, but a multiplicity of gates, at some of which clamored Forms he strove not to remember.

And then, suddenly, he felt a greater terror than that which any of the Forms could give—a terror from which he could not flee because it was connected with himself. Even the First Gateway had taken something of stability from him, leaving him uncertain about his bodily form and about his relationship to the mistily defined objects around him, but it had not disturbed his sense of unity. He had still been Randolph Carter, a fixed point in the dimensional seething. Now, beyond the Ultimate Gateway, he realized in a moment of consuming fright that he was not one person, but many persons.

He was in many places at the same time. On Earth, on October 7, 1883, a little boy named Randolph Carter was leaving the Snake Den in the hushed evening light and running down the rocky slope, and through the twisted-boughed orchard toward his Uncle Christopher's house in the hills beyond Arkham; yet at that same moment, which was also somehow in the earthly year of 1928, a vague shadow not less Randolph Carter was sitting on a pedestal among the Ancient Ones in Earth's transdimensional extension. Here, too, was a third Randolph Carter, in the unknown and formless cosmic abyss beyond the Ultimate Gate. And elsewhere, in a chaos of scenes whose infinite multiplicity and monstrous diversity brought him close to the brink of madness, were a limitless confusion of beings which he knew were as much himself as the local manifestation now beyond the Ultimate Gate.

There were Carters in settings belonging to every known and suspected age of Earth's history, and to remoter ages of earthly entity transcending knowledge, suspicion, and credibility; Carters of forms both human and non-human, vertebrate and invertebrate, conscious and mindless, animal and vegetable. And more, there were Carters having nothing in common with earthly life, but moving outrageously amidst backgrounds of other planets and systems and galaxies and cosmic continua; spores of eternal life drifting from world to world, universe to universe, yet all equally himself. Some of the glimpses recalled dreams—both faint and vivid, single and persistent—which he had had through the long years since he first began to dream; and a few possessed a haunting, fascinating and almost horrible familiarity which no earthly logic could explain.

Faced with this realization, Randolph Carter reeled in the clutch of supreme horror—horror such as had not been hinted even at the climax of that hideous night when two had ventured into an ancient and abhorred necropolis under a waning moon and only one had emerged. No death, no doom, no anguish can arouse the surpassing despair which flows from a loss of *identity*. Merging with nothingness is peaceful oblivion; but to be aware of existence and yet to know that one is no longer a definite being distinguished from other beings—that one no longer has a *self*—that is the nameless summit of agony and dread.

He knew that there had been a Randolph Carter of Boston, yet could not be sure whether he—the fragment or facet of an entity beyond the Ultimate Gate—had been that one or some other. His *self* had been annihilated; and yet he—if indeed there could, in view of that utter nullity of individual existence, be such a thing as *he*—was equally aware of being in some inconceivable way a legion of selves. It was as though his body had been suddenly transformed into one of those many-limbed and many-headed effigies sculptured in Indian temples, and he contemplated the aggregation in a bewildered attempt to discern which was the original and which the additions—if indeed (supremely monstrous thought!) there *were* any original as distinguished from other embodiments.

Then, in the midst of these devastating reflections, Carter's beyond-the-gate fragment was hurled from what had seemed the nadir of horror to black, clutching pits of a horror still more profound. This time it was largely external—a force or personality which at once confronted and surrounded and pervaded him, and which in addition to its local presence, seemed also to be a part of himself, and likewise to be co-existent with all time and conterminous with all space. There was no visual image, yet the sense of entity and the awful concept of combined localism and identity and infinity lent a paralyzing terror beyond anything which any Carter-fragment had hitherto deemed capable of existing.

In the face of that awful wonder, the quasi-Carter forgot the horror of destroyed individuality. It was an All-in-One and One-in-All of limitless being and self—not merely a thing of one space-time continuum, but allied to the ultimate animating essence of existence's whole unbounded sweep—the last, utter sweep which has no confines and which outreaches fancy and mathematics alike. It was perhaps that which certain secret cults of Earth had whispered of as *Yog-Sothoth*, and which has been a deity under other names; that which the crustaceans of Yuggoth worship as the Beyond-One, and which the vaporous brains of the spiral nebulæ know by an untranslatable sign—yet in a flash the Carter-facet realized how slight and fractional all these conceptions are.

And now the Being was addressing the Carter-facet in prodigious waves that smote and burned and thundered—a concentration of energy that blasted its recipient with well-nigh unendurable violence, and that paralleled in an unearthly rhythm the curious swaying of the Ancient Ones, and the flickering of the monstrous lights, in that baffling region beyond the First Gate. It was as though suns and worlds and universes had converged upon one point whose very position in space they had conspired to annihilate with an impact of resistless fury. But amidst the greater terror one lesser terror was diminished; for the searing waves appeared somehow to isolate the Beyond-the-Gate Carter from his infinity of duplicates—to restore, as it were, a certain amount of the illusion of identity. After a time the hearer began to translate the waves into speech-forms known to him, and his sense of horror and oppression waned. Fright became pure awe, and what had seemed blasphemously abnormal seemed now only ineffably majestic.

"Randolph Carter," it seemed to say, "my manifestations on your planet's extension, the Ancient Ones, have sent you as one who would lately have returned to small lands of dream which he had lost, yet who with greater freedom has risen to greater and nobler desires and curiosities. You wished to sail up golden Oukranos, to search out forgotten ivory cities in orchid-heavy Kled, and to reign on the opal throne of Ilek-Vad, whose fabulous towers and numberless domes rise mighty toward a single red star in a filament alien to your Earth and to all matter. Now, with the passing of two Gates, you wish loftier things.

You would not flee like a child from a scene disliked to a dream beloved, but would plunge like a man into that last and inmost of secrets which lies behind all scenes and dreams.

"What you wish, I have found good; and I am ready to grant that which I have granted eleven times only to beings of your planet—five times only to those you call men, or those resembling them. I am ready to show you the Ultimate Mystery, to look on which is to blast a feeble spirit. Yet before you gaze full at that last and first of secrets you may still wield a free choice, and return if you will through the two Gates with the Veil still unrent before your eyes."

CHAPTER 5

A sudden shutting-off of the waves left Carter in a chilling and awesome silence full of the spirit of desolation. On every hand pressed the illimitable vastness of the void; yet the seeker knew that the Being was still there. After a moment he thought of words whose mental substance he flung into the abyss: "I accept. I will not retreat."

The waves surged forth again, and Carter knew that the Being had heard. And now there poured from that limitless Mind a flood of knowledge and explanation which opened new vistas to the seeker, and prepared him for such a grasp of the cosmos as he had never hoped to possess. He was told how childish and limited is the notion of a tri-dimensional world, and what an infinity of directions there are besides the known directions of up-down, forward-backward, right-left. He was shown the smallness and tinsel emptiness of the little Earth gods, with their petty, human interests and connections—their hatreds, rages, loves and vanities; their craving for praise and sacrifice, and their demands for faiths contrary to reason and nature.

While most of the impressions translated themselves to Carter as words, there were others to which other senses gave interpretation. Perhaps with eyes and perhaps with imagination he perceived that he was in a region of dimensions beyond those conceivable to the eye and brain of man. He saw now, in the brooding shadows of that which had been first a vortex of power and then an illimitable void, a sweep of creation that dizzied his senses. From some inconceivable vantage-point he looked upon prodigious forms whose multiple extensions transcended any conception of being, size and boundaries which his mind had hitherto been able to hold, despite a lifetime of cryptical study. He began to understand dimly why there could exist at the same time the little boy Randolph Carter in the Arkham farmhouse in 1883, the misty form on the vaguely hexagonal pillar beyond the First Gate, the fragment now facing the Presence in the limitless abyss, and all the other Carters his fancy or perception envisaged.

Then the waves increased in strength and sought to improve his understanding, reconciling him to the multiform entity of which his present fragment was an infinitesimal part. They told him that every figure of space is but the result of the intersection by a plane of some corresponding figure of one more dimension—as a square is cut from a cube, or a circle from a sphere. The cube and sphere, of three dimensions, are thus cut from corresponding forms of four dimensions, which men know only through guesses and dreams; and these in turn are cut from forms of five dimensions, and so on up to the dizzy and reachless heights of archetypal infinity. The world of men and of the gods of men is merely an infinitesimal phase of an infinitesimal thing—the three-dimensional phase of that small wholeness reached by the First Gate, where Umr at-Tawil dictates dreams to the Ancient Ones. Though men hail it as reality, and brand thoughts of its many-dimensioned original as unreality, it is in truth the very opposite. That which we call substance and reality is shadow and illusion, and that which we call shadow and illusion is substance and reality.

Time, the waves went on, is motionless, and without beginning or end. That it has motion and is the cause of change is an illusion. Indeed, it is itself really an illusion, for except to the narrow sight of beings in limited dimensions there are no such things as past, present and future. Men think of time only because of what they call change, yet that too is illusion. All that was, and is, and is to be, exists simultaneously.

These revelations came with a god-like solemnity which left Carter unable to doubt. Even though they lay almost beyond his comprehension, he felt that they must be true in the light of that final cosmic reality which belies all local perspectives and narrow partial views; and he was familiar enough with profound speculations to be free from the bondage of local and partial conceptions. Had his whole quest not been based upon a faith in the unreality of the local and partial?

After an impressive pause the waves continued, saying that what the denizens of few-dimensioned zones call change is merely a function of their consciousness, which views the external world from various cosmic angles. As the Shapes produced by the cutting of a cone seem to vary with the angles of cutting—being circle, ellipse, parabola or hyperbola according to that angle, yet without any change in the cone itself—so do the local aspects of an unchanged and endless reality seem to change with the cosmic angle of regarding. To this variety of angles of consciousness the feeble beings of the inner worlds are slaves, since with rare exceptions they can not learn to control them. Only a few students of forbidden things have gained inklings of this control, and have thereby conquered time and change. But the entities outside the Gates command all angles, and view the myriad parts of the cosmos in terms of fragmentary change-involving perspective, or of the changeless totality beyond perspective, in accordance with their will.

As the waves paused again, Carter began to comprehend, vaguely and terrifiedly, the ultimate background of that riddle of lost individuality which had at first so horrified him. His intuition pieced together the fragments of revelation, and brought him closer and closer to a grasp of the secret. He understood that much of the frightful revelation would have come upon him—splitting up his ego amongst myriads of earthly counterparts—inside the First Gate, had not the magic of 'Umr at-Tawil kept it from him in order that he might use the silver key with precision for the Ultimate Gate's opening. Anxious for clearer knowledge, he sent out waves of thought, asking more of the exact relationship between his various facets—the fragment now beyond the Ultimate Gate, the fragment still on the quasi-hexagonal pedestal beyond the First Gate, the boy of 1883, the man of 1928, the various ancestral beings who had formed his heritage and the bulwark of his ego, and the nameless denizens of the other eons and other worlds which that first hideous flash of ultimate perception had identified with him. Slowly the waves of the Being surged out in reply, trying to make plain what was almost beyond the reach of an earthly mind.

All descended lines of beings of the finite dimensions, continued the waves, and all stages of growth in each one of these beings, are merely manifestations of one archetypal and eternal being in the space outside dimensions. Each local being—son, father, grandfather, and so on—and each stage of individual being—infant, child, boy, man—is merely one of the infinite phases of that same archetypal and eternal being, caused by a variation in the angle of the consciousness-plane which cuts it. Randolph Carter at all ages; Randolph Carter and all his ancestors, both human and pre-human, terrestrial and pre-terrestrial; all these were only phases of one ultimate, eternal "Carter" outside space and time—phantom projections differentiated only by the angle at which the plane of consciousness happened to cut the eternal archetype in each case.

A slight change of angle could turn the student of today into the child of yesterday; could turn Randolph Carter into that wizard, Edmund Carter who fled from Salem to the hills behind Arkham in 1692, or that Pickman Carter who in the year 2169 would use strange means in repelling the Mongol hordes from Australia; could turn a human Carter into one of those earlier entities which had dwelt in primal Hyperborea and worshipped black, plastic Tsathoggua after flying down from Kythamil, the double planet that once revolved around Arcturus; could turn a terrestrial Carter to a remotely ancestral and doubtfully shaped dweller on Kythamil itself, or a still remoter creature of trans-galactic Stronti, or a four-dimensioned gaseous consciousness in an older space-time continuum, or a vegetable brain of the future on a dark, radio-active comet of inconceivable orbit—and so on, in endless cosmic cycle.

The archetypes, throbbed the waves, are the people of the Ultimate Abyss—formless, ineffable, and guessed at only by rare dreamers on the low-dimensioned worlds. Chief among such was this informing Being itself ... *which indeed was Carter's own archetype.* The glutless zeal of Carter and all his forebears for forbidden cosmic secrets was a natural result of derivation from the Supreme Archetype. On every world all great wizards, all great thinkers, all great artists, are facets of It.

Almost stunned with awe, and with a kind of terrifying delight, Randolph Carter's consciousness did homage to that transcendent Entity from which it was derived. As the waves paused again he pondered in the mighty silence, thinking of strange tributes, stranger questions, and still stranger requests. Curious concepts flowed conflictingly through a brain dazed with unaccustomed vistas and unforeseen disclosures. It occurred to him that, if these disclosures were literally true, he might bodily visit all those infinitely distant ages and parts of the universe which he had hitherto known only in dreams, could he but command the magic to change the angle of his consciousness-plane. And did not the silver key supply that magic? Had it not first changed him from a man in 1928 to a boy in 1883, and then to something quite outside time? Oddly, despite his present apparent absence of body, he knew that the key was still with him.

While the silence still lasted, Randolph Carter radiated forth the thoughts and questions which assailed him. He knew that in this ultimate abyss he was equidistant from every facet of his archetype—human or non-human, terrestrial or extra-terrestrial, galactic or trans-galactic; and his curiosity regarding the other phases of his being—especially those phases which were farthest from an earthly 1928 in time and space, or which had most persistently haunted his dreams throughout life—was at fever heat. He felt that his archetypal Entity could at will send him bodily to any of these phases of bygone and distant life by changing his consciousness-plane, and despite the marvels he had undergone he burned for the further marvel of walking in the flesh through those grotesque and incredible scenes which visions of the night had fragmentarily brought him.

Without definite intention he was asking the Presence for access to a dim, fantastic world whose five multicolored suns, alien constellations, dizzily black crags, clawed, tapir-snouted denizens, bizarre metal towers, unexplained tunnels, and cryptical floating cylinders had intruded again and again upon his slumbers. That world, he felt vaguely, was in all the conceivable cosmos the one most freely in touch with others; and he longed to explore the vistas whose beginnings he had glimpsed, and to embark through space to those still remoter worlds with which the clawed, snouted denizens trafficked. There was no time for fear. As at all crises of his strange life, sheer cosmic curiosity triumphed over everything else.

When the waves resumed their awesome pulsing, Carter knew that his terrible request was granted. The Being was telling him of the nighted gulfs through which he would have to pass, of the unknown quintuple star in an unsuspected galaxy around which the alien world revolved, and of the burrowing inner horrors against which the clawed, snouted race of that world perpetually fought. It told him, too, of how the angle of his personal consciousness-plane, and the angle of his consciousness-plane regarding the space-time elements of the sought for world, would have to be tilted simultaneously in order to restore to that world the Carter-facet which had dwelt there.

The Presence warned him to be sure of his symbols if he wished ever to return from the remote and alien world he had chosen, and he radiated back an impatient affirmation; confident that the silver key, which he felt was with him and which he knew had tilted both world and personal planes in throwing him back to 1883, contained those symbols which were meant. And now the Being, grasping his impatience, signified its readiness to accomplish the monstrous precipitation. The waves abruptly ceased, and there supervened a momentary stillness tense with nameless and dreadful expectancy.

Then, without warning, came a whirring and drumming that swelled to a terrific thundering. Once again Carter felt himself the focal point of an intense concentration of energy which smote and hammered and seared unbearably in the now-familiar rhythm of outer space, and which he could not classify as either the blasting heat of a blazing star, or the all-petrifying cold of the ultimate abyss. Bands and rays of color utterly foreign to any spectrum of our universe played and wove and interlaced before him, and he was conscious of a frightful velocity of motion. He caught one fleeting glimpse of a figure sitting *alone* upon a cloudy throne more hexagonal than otherwise....

CHAPTER 6

As the Hindoo paused in his story he saw that de Marigny and Phillips were watching him absorbedly. Aspinwall pretended to ignore the narrative and kept his eyes ostentatiously on the papers before him. The alien-rhythmed ticking of the coffin-shaped clock took on a new and portentous meaning, while the fumes from the choked, neglected tripods wove themselves into fantastic and inexplicable shapes, and formed disturbing combinations with the grotesque figures of the draft-swayed tapestries. The old negro who had tended them was gone—perhaps some growing tension had frightened him out of the house. An almost apologetic hesitancy hampered the speaker as he resumed in his oddly labored yet idiomatic voice.

"You have found these things of the abyss hard to believe," he said, "but you will find the tangible and material things ahead still harder. That is the way of our minds. Marvels are doubly incredible when brought into three dimensions from the vague regions of possible dream. I shall not try to tell you much—that would be another and very different story. I will tell only what you absolutely have to know."

Carter, after that final vortex of alien and polychromatic rhythm, had found himself in what for a moment he thought was his old insistent dream. He was, as many a night before, walking amidst throngs of clawed, snouted beings through the streets of a labyrinth of inexplicably fashioned metal under a blaze of diverse solar color; and as he looked down he saw that his body was like those of the others—rugose, partly squamous, and curiously articulated in a fashion mainly insect-like yet not without a caricaturish resemblance to the human outline. The silver key was still in his grasp, though held by a noxious-looking claw.

In another moment the dream-sense vanished, and he felt rather as one just awakened from a dream. The ultimate abyss—the Being—the entity of absurd, outlandish race called Randolph Carter on a world of the future not yet born—some of these things were parts of the persistent recurrent dreams of the wizard Zkauba on the planet Yaddith. They were too persistent—they interfered with his duties in weaving spells to keep the frightful Dholes in their burrows, and became mixed up with his recollections of the myriad real worlds he had visited in light-beam envelopes. And now they had become quasi-real as never before. This heavy, material silver key in his right upper claw, exact image of one he had dreamt about, meant no good. He must rest and reflect, and consult the tablets of Nhing for advice on what to do. Climbing a metal wall in a lane off the main concourse, he entered his apartment and approached the rack of tablets.

Seven day-fractions later Zkauba squatted on his prism in awe and half despair, for the truth had opened up a new and conflicting set of memories. Nevermore could he know the peace of being one entity. For all time and space he was two: Zkauba the wizard of Yaddith, disgusted with the thought of the repellent earth-mammal Carter that he was to be and had been, and Randolph Carter, of Boston on the Earth, shivering with fright at the clawed, snouted thing which he had once been, and had become again.

The time units spent on Yaddith, croaked the Swami—whose labored voice was beginning to show signs of fatigue—

made a tale in themselves which could not be related in brief compass. There were trips to Stronti and Mthura and Kath, and other worlds in the twenty-eight galaxies accessible to the light-beam envelopes of the creatures of Yaddith, and trips back and forth through eons of time with the aid of the silver key and various other symbols known to Yaddith's wizards. There were hideous struggles with the bleached viscous Dholes in the primal tunnels that honeycombed the planet. There were awed sessions in libraries amongst the massed lore of ten thousand worlds living and dead. There were tense conferences with other minds of Yaddith, including that of the Arch-Ancient Buo. Zkauba told no one of what had befallen his personality, but when the Randolph Carter facet was uppermost he would study furiously every possible means of returning to the Earth and to human form, and would desperately practise human speech with the alien throat-organs so ill adapted to it.

The Carter-facet had soon learned with horror that the silver key was unable to effect his return to human form. It was, as he deduced too late from things he remembered, things he dreamed, and things he inferred from the lore of Yaddith, a product of Hyperborea on Earth; with power over the personal consciousness-angles of human beings alone. It could, however, change the planetary angle and send the user at will through time in an unchanged body. There had been an added spell which gave it limitless powers it otherwise lacked; but this, too, was a human discovery—peculiar to a spatially unreachable region, and not to be duplicated by the wizards of Yaddith. It had been written on the undecipherable parchment in the hideously carven box with the silver key, and Carter bitterly lamented that he had left it behind. The now inaccessible Being of the abyss had warned him to be sure of his symbols, and had doubtless thought he lacked nothing.

As time wore on he strove harder and harder to utilize the monstrous lore of Yaddith in finding a way back to the abyss and the omnipotent Entity. With his new knowledge he could have done much toward reading the cryptic parchment; but that power, under present conditions, was merely ironic. There were times, however, when the Zkauba-facet was uppermost, and when he strove to erase the conflicting Carter-memories which troubled him.

Thus long spaces of time wore on—ages longer than the brain of man could grasp, since the beings of Yaddith die only after prolonged cycles. After many hundreds of revolutions the Carter-facet seemed to gain on the Zkauba-facet, and would spend vast periods calculating the distance of Yaddith in space and time from the human Earth that was to be. The figures were staggering—eons of light-years beyond counting—but the immemorial lore of Yaddith fitted Carter to grasp such things. He cultivated the power of dreaming himself momentarily Earthward, and learned many things about our planet that he had never known before. But he could not dream the needed formula on the missing parchment.

Then at last he conceived a wild plan of escape from Yaddith—which began when he found a drug that would keep his Zkauba-facet always dormant, yet without dissolution of the knowledge and memories of Zkauba. He thought that his calculations would let him perform a voyage with a light-wave envelope such as no being of Yaddith had ever performed—a *bodily* voyage through nameless eons and across incredible galactic reaches to the solar system and the Earth itself. Once on Earth, though in the body of a clawed, snouted thing, he might be able somehow to find—and finish deciphering—the strangely hieroglyphed parchment he had left in the car at Arkham; and with its aid—and the key's—resume his normal terrestrial semblance.

He was not blind to the perils of the attempt. He knew that when he had brought the planet-angle to the right eon (a thing impossible to do while hurtling through space), Yaddith would be a dead world dominated by triumphant Dholes, and that his escape in the light-wave envelope would be a matter of grave doubt. Likewise was he aware of how he must achieve suspended animation, in the manner of an adept, to endure the eon-long flight through fathomless abysses. He knew, too, that—assuming his voyage succeeded—he must immunize himself to the bacterial and other earthly conditions hostile to a body from Yaddith. Furthermore, he must provide a way of feigning human shape on Earth until he might recover and decipher the parchment and resume that shape in truth. Otherwise he would probably be discovered and destroyed by the people in horror as a thing that should not be. And there must be some gold—luckily obtainable on Yaddith—to tide him over that period of quest.

Slowly Carter's plans went forward. He provided a light-wave envelope of abnormal toughness, able to stand both the prodigious time-transition and the unexampled flight through space. He tested all his calculations, and sent forth his Earthward dreams again and again, bringing them as close as possible to 1928. He practised suspended animation with marvelous success. He discovered just the bacterial agent he needed, and worked out the varying gravity-stress to which he must become used. He artfully fashioned a waxen mask and loose costume enabling him to pass among men as a human being of a sort, and devised a doubly potent spell with which to hold back the Dholes at the moment of his starting from the dead, black Yaddith of the inconceivable future. He took care, too, to assemble a large supply of the drugs—unobtainable on Earth—which would keep his Zkauba-facet in abeyance till he might shed the Yaddith body, nor did he neglect a small store of gold for earthly use.

The starting-day was a time of doubt and apprehension. Carter climbed up to his envelope-platform, on the pretext of sailing for the triple star Nython, and crawled into the sheath of shining metal. He had just room to perform the ritual of the silver key, and as he did so he slowly started the levitation of his envelope. There was an appalling seething and darkening of the day, and a hideous racking of pain. The cosmos seemed to reel irresponsibly, and the other constellations danced in a black sky.

"Below him the ground was festering with gigantic Dholes."

All at once Carter felt a new equilibrium. The cold of interstellar gulfs gnawed at the outside of his envelope, and he could see that he floated free in space—the metal building from which he had started having decayed years before. Below him the ground was festering with gigantic Dholes; and even as he looked, one reared up several hundred feet and levelled a bleached, viscous end at him. But his spells were effective, and in another moment he was falling away from Yaddith, unharmed.

CHAPTER 7

In that bizarre room in New Orleans, from which the old black servant had instinctively fled, the odd voice of Swami Chandraputra grew hoarser still.

"Gentlemen," he continued, "I will not ask you to believe these things until I have shown you special proof. Accept it, then, as a myth, when I tell you of the *thousands of light-years—thousands of years of time, and uncounted billions of miles* that Randolph Carter hurtled through space as a nameless, alien entity in a thin envelope of electron-activated metal. He timed his period of suspended animation with utmost care, planning to have it end only a few years before the time of landing on the Earth in or near 1928.

"He will never forget that awakening. Remember, gentlemen, that before that eon-long sleep *he had lived consciously for thousands of terrestrial years amidst the alien and horrible wonders of Yaddith.* There was a hideous gnawing of cold, a cessation of menacing dreams, and a glance through the eye-plates of the envelope. Stars, clusters, nebulæ, on every hand—*and at last their outlines bore some kinship to the constellations of Earth that he knew.*

"Some day his descent into the solar system may be told. He saw Kynarth and Yuggoth on the rim, passed close to Neptune and glimpsed the hellish white fungi that spot it, learned an untellable secret from the close-glimpsed mists of Jupiter, and saw the horror on one of the satellites, and gazed at the cyclopean ruins that sprawl over Mars' ruddy disk. When the Earth drew near he saw it as a thin crescent which swelled alarmingly in size. He slackened speed, though his sensations of homecoming made him wish to lose not a moment. I will not try to tell you of those sensations as I learned them from Carter.

"Well, toward the last Carter hovered about in the Earth's upper air waiting till daylight came over the Western Hemisphere. He wanted to land where he had left—near the Snake Den in the hills behind Arkham. If any of you have been away from home long—and I know one of you has—I leave it to you how the sight of New England's rolling hills and great elms and gnarled orchards and ancient stone walls must have affected him.

"He came down at dawn in the lower meadow of the old Carter place, and was thankful for the silence and solitude. It was autumn, as when he had left, and the smell of the hills was balm to his soul. He managed to drag the metal envelope up the slope of the timber-lot into the Snake Den, though it would not go through the weed-choked fissure to the inner cave. It was there also that he covered his alien body with the human clothing and waxen mask which would be necessary. He kept the envelope here for over a year, till certain circumstances made a new hiding-place necessary.

"He walked to Arkham—incidentally practising the management of his body in human posture and against terrestrial gravity—and got his gold changed to money at a bank. He also made some inquiries—posing as a foreigner ignorant of much English—and found that the year was 1930, only two years after the goal he had aimed at.

"Of course, his position was horrible. Unable to assert his identity, forced to live on guard every moment, with certain difficulties regarding food, and with a need to conserve the alien drug which kept his Zkauba-facet dormant, he felt that he must act as quickly as possible. Going to Boston and taking a room in the decaying West End, where he could live cheaply and inconspicuously, he at once established inquiries concerning Randolph Carter's estate and effects. It was then that he learned how anxious Mr. Aspinwall, here, was to have the estate divided, and how valiantly Mr. de Marigny and Mr. Phillips strove to keep it intact."

The Hindoo bowed, though no expression crossed his dark, tranquil, and thickly bearded face.

"Indirectly," he continued, "Carter secured a good copy of the missing parchment and began working on its deciphering. I am glad to say that I was able to help in all this—for he appealed to me quite early, and through me came in touch with other mystics throughout the world. I went to live with him in Boston—a wretched place in Chambers Street. As for the parchment—I am pleased to help Mr. de Marigny in his perplexity. To him let me say that the language of those hieroglyphics is not Naacal, but R'lyehian, which was brought to Earth by the spawn of Cthulhu countless ages ago. It is, of course, a translation—there was an Hyperborean original millions of years earlier in the primal tongue of Tsath-yo.

"There was more to decipher than Carter had looked for, but at no time did he give up hope. Early this year he made great strides through a book he imported from Nepal, and there is no question but that he will win before long. Unfortunately, however, one handicap has developed—the exhaustion of the alien drug which keeps the Zkauba-facet dormant. This is not, however, as great a calamity as was feared. Carter's personality is gaining in the body, and when Zkauba comes uppermost—for shorter and shorter periods, and now only when evoked by some unusual excitement—he is generally too dazed to undo any of Carter's work. He can not find the metal envelope that would take him back to Yaddith, for although he almost did, once, Carter hid it anew at a time when the Zkauba-facet was wholly latent. All the harm he has done is to frighten a few people and create certain nightmare rumors among the Poles and Lithuanians of Boston's West End. So far, he has never injured the careful disguise prepared by the Carter-facet, though he sometimes throws it off so that parts have to be replaced. I have seen what lies beneath—and it is not good to see.

"A month ago Carter saw the advertisement of this meeting, and knew that he must act quickly to save his estate. He could not wait to decipher the parchment and resume his human form. Consequently he deputed me to act for him.

"Gentlemen, I say to you that Randolph Carter is not dead; that he is temporarily in an anomalous condition, but that within two or three months at the outside he will be able to appear in proper form and demand the custody of his estate. I am prepared to offer proof if necessary. Therefore I beg that you will adjourn this meeting for an indefinite period."

CHAPTER 8

De Marigny and Phillips stared at the Hindoo as if hypnotized, while Aspinwall emitted a series of snorts and bellows. The old attorney's disgust had by now surged into open rage, and he pounded the table with an apoplectically veined fist. When he spoke, it was in a kind of bark.

"How long is this foolery to be borne? I've listened an hour to this madman—this faker—and now he has the damned effrontery to say Randolph Carter is alive—to ask us to postpone the settlement for no good reason! Why don't you throw the scoundrel out, de Marigny? Do you mean to make us all the butts of a charlatan or idiot?"

De Marigny quietly raised his hand and spoke softly.

"Let us think slowly and clearly. This has been a very singular tale, and there are things in it which I, as a mystic not altogether ignorant, recognize as far from impossible. Furthermore—since 1930 I have received letters from the Swami which tally with his account."

As he paused, old Mr. Phillips ventured a word.

"Swami Chandraputra spoke of proofs. I, too, recognize much that is significant in this story, and I have myself had many oddly corroborative letters from the Swami during the last two years; but some of these statements are very extreme. Is there not something tangible which can be shown?"

At last the impassive-faced Swami replied, slowly and hoarsely, and drawing an object from the pocket of his loose coat as he spoke.

"While none of you here has ever *seen* the silver key itself, Messrs. de Marigny and Phillips have seen photographs of it. *Does this look familiar to you?*"

He fumblingly laid on the table, with his large, white-mittened hand, a heavy key of tarnished silver—nearly five inches long, of unknown and utterly exotic workmanship, and covered from end to end with hieroglyphs of the most bizarre description. De Marigny and Phillips gasped.

"That's it!" cried de Marigny. "The camera doesn't lie. I couldn't be mistaken!"

But Aspinwall had already launched a reply.

"Fools! What does it prove? If that's really the key that belonged to my cousin, it's up to this foreigner—this damned nigger—to explain how he got it! Randolph Carter vanished with the key four years ago. How do we know he wasn't robbed and murdered? He was half crazy himself, and in touch with still crazier people.

"Look here, you nigger—where did you get that key? Did you kill Randolph Carter?"

The Swami's features, abnormally placid, did not change; but the remote, irisless black eyes behind them blazed dangerously. He spoke with great difficulty.

"Please control yourself, Mr. Aspinwall. There is another form of proof that I *could* give, but its effect upon everybody would not be pleasant. Let us be reasonable. Here are some papers obviously written since 1930, and in the unmistakable style of Randolph Carter."

He clumsily drew a long envelope from inside his loose coat and handed it to the sputtering attorney as de Marigny and Phillips watched with chaotic thoughts and a dawning feeling of supernal wonder.

"Of course the handwriting is almost illegible—but remember that Randolph Carter now has no hands well adapted to forming human script."

Aspinwall looked through the papers hurriedly, and was visibly perplexed, but he did not change his demeanor. The room was tense with excitement and nameless dread, and the alien rhythm of the coffin-shaped clock had an utterly diabolic sound to de Marigny and Phillips, though the lawyer seemed affected not at all.

Aspinwall spoke again. "These look like clever forgeries. If they aren't, they may mean that Randolph Carter has been brought under the control of people with no good purpose. There's only one thing to do—have this faker arrested. De Marigny, will you telephone for the police?"

"Let us wait," answered their host. "I do not think this case calls for the police. I have a certain idea. Mr. Aspinwall, this gentleman is a mystic of real attainments. He says he is in the confidence of Randolph Carter. Will it satisfy you if he can answer certain questions which could be answered only by one in such confidence? I know Carter, and can ask such questions. Let me get a book which I think will make a good test."

He turned toward the door to the library, Phillips dazedly following in a kind of automatic way. Aspinwall remained where he was, studying closely the Hindoo who confronted him with abnormally impassive face. Suddenly, as Chandraputra clumsily restored the silver key to his pocket, the lawyer emitted a guttural shout.

"Hey, by Heaven! I've got it! This rascal is in disguise. I don't believe he's an East Indian at all. That face—it isn't a face, but a *mask*! I guess his story put that into my head, but it's true. It never moves, and that turban and beard hide the edges. This fellow's a common crook! He isn't even a foreigner—I've been watching his language. He's a Yankee of some sort. And look at those mittens—he knows his fingerprints could be spotted. Damn you, I'll pull that thing off—"

"Stop!" The hoarse, oddly alien voice of the Swami held a tone beyond all mere earthly fright. "I told you there was *another form of proof which I could give if necessary*, and I warned you not to provoke me to it. This red-faced old meddler is right—I'm not really an East Indian. *This face is a mask, and what it covers is not human.* You others have guessed—I felt that minutes ago. It wouldn't be pleasant if I took that mask off—let it alone, Ernest. I may as well tell you that *I am Randolph Carter.*"

No one moved. Aspinwall snorted and made vague motions. De Marigny and Phillips, across the room, watched the workings of the red face and studied the back of the turbaned figure that confronted him. The clock's abnormal ticking was hideous, and the tripod fumes and swaying arras danced a dance of death. The half-choking lawyer broke the silence.

"No you don't, you crook—you can't scare me! You've reasons of your own for not wanting that mask off. Maybe we'd know who you are. Off with it—"

As he reached forward, the Swami seized his hand with one of his own clumsily mittened members, evoking a curious cry of mixed pain and surprize. De Marigny started toward the two, but paused confused as the pseudo-Hindoo's shout of protest changed to a wholly inexplicable rattling and buzzing sound. Aspinwall's red face was furious, and with his free hand he made another lunge at his opponent's bushy beard. This time he succeeded in getting a hold, and at his frantic tug the whole waxen visage came loose from the turban and clung to the lawyer's apoplectic fist.

As it did so, Aspinwall uttered a frightful gurgling cry, and Phillips and de Marigny saw his face convulsed with a wilder, deeper and more hideous epilepsy of stark panic than ever they had seen on human countenance before. The pseudo-Swami had meanwhile released his other hand and was standing as if dazed, making buzzing noises of a most abnormal quality. Then the turbaned figure slumped oddly into a posture scarcely human, and began a curious, fascinated sort of shuffle toward the coffin-shaped clock that ticked out its cosmic and abnormal rhythm. His now uncovered face was turned away, and de Marigny and Phillips could not see what the lawyer's act had disclosed. Then their attention was turned to Aspinwall, who was sinking ponderously to the floor. The spell was broken—but when they reached the old man he was dead.

Turning quickly to the shuffling Swami's receding back, de Marigny saw one of the great white mittens drop listlessly off a dangling arm. The fumes of the olibanum were thick, and all that could be glimpsed of the revealed hand was something long and black. Before the Creole could reach the retreating figure, old Mr. Phillips laid a restraining hand on his shoulder.

"Don't!" he whispered. "We don't know what we're up against. That other facet, you know—Zkauba, the wizard of Yaddith...."

The turbaned figure had now reached the abnormal clock, and the watchers saw through the dense fumes a blurred black claw fumbling with the tall, hieroglyphed door. The fumbling made a queer, clicking sound. Then the figure entered the coffin-shaped case and pulled the door shut after it.

De Marigny could no longer be restrained, but when he reached and opened the clock it was empty. The abnormal ticking went on, beating out the dark, cosmic rhythm which underlies all mystical gate-openings. On the floor the great white mitten, and the dead man with a bearded mask clutched in his hand, had nothing further to reveal.

A year passed, and nothing has been heard of Randolph Carter. His estate is still unsettled. The Boston address from which one "Swami Chandraputra" sent inquiries to various mystics in 1930-31-32 was indeed tenanted by a strange Hindoo, but he left shortly before the date of the New Orleans conference and has never been seen since. He was said to be dark, expressionless, and bearded, and his landlord thinks the swarthy mask—which was duly exhibited—looks very much like him. He was never, however, suspected of any connection with the nightmare apparitions whispered of by local Slavs. The hills behind Arkham were searched for the "metal envelope," but nothing of the sort was ever found. However, a clerk in Arkham's First National Bank does recall a queer turbaned man who cashed an odd bit of gold bullion in October, 1930.

De Marigny and Phillips scarcely know what to make of the business. After all, what was proved? There was a story. There was a key which might have been forged from one of the pictures Carter had freely distributed in 1928. There were papers—all indecisive. There was a masked stranger, but who now living saw behind the mask? Amidst the strain and the olibanum fumes that act of vanishing in the clock might easily have been a dual hallucination. Hindoos know much of hypnotism. Reason proclaims the "Swami" a criminal with designs on Randolph Carter's estate. But the autopsy said that Aspinwall had died of shock. Was it rage *alone* which caused it? And some things in that story....

In a vast room hung with strangely figured arras and filled with olibanum fumes, Etienne-Laurent de Marigny often sits listening with vague sensations to the abnormal rhythm of that hieroglyphed, coffin-shaped clock.